Hellhounds of the Cosmos

Hellhounds of the Cosmos
by Clifford D. Simak

The paper had gone to press, graphically describing the latest of the many horrible events which had been enacted upon the Earth in the last six months. The headlines screamed that Six Corners, a little hamlet in Pennsylvania, had been wiped out by the Horror. Another front-page story told of a Terror in the Amazon Valley which had sent the natives down the river in babbling fear. Other stories told of deaths here and there, all attributable to the "Black Horror," as it was called.

The telephone rang.

"Hello," said the editor.

"London calling," came the voice of the operator.

"All right," replied the editor.

He recognized the voice of Terry Masters, special correspondent. His voice came clearly over the transatlantic telephone.

"The Horror is attacking London in force," he said. "There are thousands of them and they have completely surrounded the city. All roads are blocked. The government declared the city under martial rule a quarter of an hour ago and efforts are being made to prepare for resistance against the enemy."

"Just a second," the editor shouted into the transmitter.

He touched a button on his desk and in a moment an answering buzz told him he was in communication with the press-room.

"Stop the presses!" he yelled into the speaking tube. "Get ready for a new front make-up!"

"O.K.," came faintly through the tube, and the editor turned back to the phone.

"Now let's have it," he said, and the voice at the London end of the wire droned on, telling the story that in another half hour was read by a world which shuddered in cold fear even as it scanned the glaring headlines.

"Woods," said the editor of the Press to a reporter, "run over and talk to Dr. Silas White. He phoned me to send someone. Something about this Horror business."

Henry Woods rose from his chair without a word and walked from the office. As he passed the wire machine it was tapping out, with a maddeningly methodical slowness, the story of the fall of London. Only half an hour before it had rapped forth the flashes concerning the attack on Paris and Berlin.

He passed out of the building into a street that was swarming with terrified humanity. Six months of terror, of numerous mysterious deaths, of villages blotted out, had set the world on edge. Now with London in possession of the Horror and Paris and

Berlin fighting hopelessly for their lives, the entire population of the world was half insane with fright.

Exhorters on street corners enlarged upon the end of the world, asking that the people prepare for eternity, attributing the Horror to the act of a Supreme Being enraged with the wickedness of the Earth.

Expecting every moment an attack by the Horror, people left their work and gathered in the streets. Traffic, in places, had been blocked for hours and law and order were practically paralyzed. Commerce and transportation were disrupted as fright-ridden people fled from the larger cities, seeking doubtful hiding places in rural districts from the death that stalked the land.

A loudspeaker in front of a music store blared forth the latest news flashes.

"It has been learned," came the measured tones of the announcer, "that all communication with Berlin ceased about ten minutes ago. At Paris all efforts to hold the Horror at bay have been futile. Explosives blow it apart, but have the same effect upon it as explosion has on gas. It flies apart and then reforms again, not always in the same shape as it was before. A new gas, one of the most deadly ever conceived by man, has failed to have any effect on the things. Electric guns and heat guns have absolutely no effect upon them.

"A news flash which has just come in from Rome says that a large number of the Horrors has been sighted north of that city by airmen. It seems they are attacking the capitals of the world first. Word comes from Washington that every known form of defense is being amassed at that city. New York is also preparing...."

Henry Woods fought his way through the crowd which milled in front of the loudspeaker. The hum of excitement was giving away to a silence, the silence of a stunned people, the fearful silence of a populace facing a presence it is unable to understand, an embattled world standing with useless weapons before an incomprehensible enemy.

In despair the reporter looked about for a taxi, but realized, with a groan of resignation, that no taxi could possibly operate in that crowded street. A street car, blocked by the stream of humanity which jostled and elbowed about it, stood still, a defeated thing.

Seemingly the only man with a definite purpose in that whirlpool of terror-stricken men and women, the newspaperman settled down to the serious business of battling his way through the swarming street.

"Before I go to the crux of the matter," said Dr. Silas White, about half an hour later, "let us first review what we know of this so-called Horror. Suppose you tell me exactly what you know of it."

Henry Woods shifted uneasily in his chair. Why didn't the old fool get down to business? The chief would raise hell if this story didn't make the regular edition. He stole a glance at his wrist-watch. There was still almost an hour left. Maybe he could manage it. If the old chap would only snap into it!

"I know no more," he said, "than is common knowledge."

The gimlet eyes of the old white-haired scientist regarded the newspaperman sharply.

"And that is?" he questioned.

There was no way out of it, thought Henry. He'd have to humor the old fellow.

"The Horror," he replied, "appeared on Earth, so far as the knowledge of man is concerned, about six months ago."

Dr. White nodded approvingly.

"You state the facts very aptly," he said.

"How so?"

"When you say 'so far as the knowledge of man is concerned.'"

"Why is that?"

"You will understand in due time. Please proceed."

Vaguely the newspaperman wondered whether he was interviewing the scientist or the scientist interviewing him.

"They were first reported," Woods said, "early this spring. At that time they wiped out a small village in the province of Quebec. All the inhabitants, except a few fugitives, were found dead, killed mysteriously and half eaten, as if by wild beasts. The fugitives were demented, babbling of black shapes that swept down out of the dark forest upon the little town in the small hours of the morning.

"The next that was heard of them was about a week later, when they struck in an isolated rural district in Poland, killing and feeding on the population of several farms. In the next week more villages were wiped out, in practically every country on the face of the Earth. From the hinterlands came tales of murder done at midnight, of men and women horribly mangled, of livestock slaughtered, of buildings crushed as if by some titanic force.

"At first they worked only at night and then, seeming to become bolder and more numerous, attacked in broad daylight."

The newspaperman paused.

"Is that what you want?" he asked.

"That's part of it," replied Dr. White, "but that's not all. What do these Horrors look like?"

"That's more difficult," said Henry. "They have been reported as every conceivable sort of monstrosity. Some are large and others are small. Some take the form of animals, others of birds and reptiles, and some are cast in appalling shapes such as might be snatched out of the horrid imagery of a thing which resided in a world entirely alien to our own."

Dr. White rose from his chair and strode across the room to confront the other.

"Young man," he asked, "do you think it possible the Horror might have come out of a world entirely alien to our own?"

"I don't know," replied Henry. "I know that some of the scientists believe they came from some other planet, perhaps even from some other solar system. I know they are like nothing ever known before on Earth. They are always inky black, something like black tar, you know, sort of sticky-looking, a disgusting sight. The weapons of mankind can't affect them. Explosives are useless and so are projectiles. They wade through poison gas and fiery chemicals and seem to enjoy them. Elaborate electrical barriers have failed. Heat doesn't make them turn a hair."

"And you think they came from some other planet, perhaps some other solar system?"

"I don't know what to think," said Henry. "If they came out of space they must have come in some conveyance, and that would certainly have been sighted, picked up long before it arrived, by our astronomers. If they came in small conveyances, there must have been many of them. If they came in a single conveyance, it would be too large to escape detection. That is, unless—"

"Unless what?" snapped the scientist.

"Unless it traveled at the speed of light. Then it would have been invisible."

"Not only invisible," snorted the old man, "but non-existent."

A question was on the tip of the newspaperman's tongue, but before it could be asked the old man was speaking again, asking a question:

"Can you imagine a fourth dimension?"

"No, I can't," said Henry.

"Can you imagine a thing of only two dimensions?"

"Vaguely, yes."

The scientist smote his palms together.

"Now we're coming to it!" he exclaimed.

Henry Woods regarded the other narrowly. The old man must be turned. What did fourth and second dimensions have to do with the Horror?

"Do you know anything about evolution?" questioned the old man.

"I have a slight understanding of it. It is the process of upward growth, the stairs by which simple organisms climb to become more complex organisms."

Dr. White grunted and asked still another question:

"Do you know anything about the theory of the exploding universe? Have you ever noted the tendency of the perfectly balanced to run amuck?"

The reporter rose slowly to his feet.

"Dr. White," he said, "you phoned my paper you had a story for us. I came here to get it, but all you have done is ask me questions. If you can't tell me what you want us to publish, I will say good-day."

The doctor put forth a hand that shook slightly.

"Sit down, young man," he said. "I don't blame you for being impatient, but I will now come to my point."

The newspaperman sat down again.

"I have developed a hypothesis," said Dr. White, "and have conducted several experiments which seem to bear it out. I am staking my reputation upon the supposition that it is correct. Not only that, but I am also staking the lives of several brave men who believe implicitly in me and my theory. After all, I suppose it makes little difference, for if I fail the world is doomed, if I succeed it is saved from complete destruction.

"Have you ever thought that our evolutionists might be wrong, that evolution might be downward instead of upward? The theory of the exploding universe, the belief that all of creation is running down, being thrown off balance by the loss of energy, spurred onward by cosmic accidents which tend to disturb its equilibrium, to a time when it will run wild and space will be filled with swirling dust of disintegrated worlds, would bear out this contention.

"This does not apply to the human race. There is no question that our evolution is upward, that we have arisen from one-celled creatures wallowing in the slime of primal seas. Our case is probably paralleled by thousands of other intelligences on far-flung planets and island universes. These instances, however, running at cross purposes to the general evolutional trend of the entire cosmos, are mere flashes in the eventual course of cosmic evolution, comparing no more to eternity than a split second does to a million years.

"Taking these instances, then, as inconsequential, let us say that the trend of cosmic evolution is downward rather than upward, from complex units to simpler units rather than from simple units to more complex ones.

"Let us say that life and intelligence have degenerated. How would you say such a degeneration would take place? In just what way would it be manifested? What sort of transition would life pass through in passing from one stage to a lower one? Just what would be the nature of these stages?"

The scientist's eyes glowed brightly as he bent forward in his chair. The newspaperman said simply: "I have no idea."

"Man," cried the old man, "can't you see that it would be a matter of dimensions? From the fourth dimension to the third, from the third to the second, from the second to the first, from the first to a questionable existence or plane which is beyond our understanding or perhaps to oblivion and the end of life. Might not the fourth have evolved from a fifth, the fifth from a sixth, the sixth from a seventh, and so on to no one knows what multidimension?"

Dr. White paused to allow the other man to grasp the importance of his statements. Woods failed lamentably to do so.

"But what has this to do with the Horror?" he asked.

"Have you absolutely no imagination?" shouted the old man.

"Why, I suppose I have, but I seem to fail to understand."

"We are facing an invasion of fourth-dimensional creatures," the old man whispered, almost as if fearful to speak the words aloud. "We are being attacked by life which is one dimension above us in evolution. We are fighting, I tell you, a tribe of hellhounds out of the cosmos. They are unthinkably above us in the matter of intelligence. There is a chasm of knowledge between us so wide and so deep that it staggers the imagination. They regard us as mere animals, perhaps not even that. So far as they are concerned we are just fodder, something to be eaten as we eat vegetables and cereals or the flesh of domesticated animals.

Perhaps they have watched us for years, watching life on the world increase, lapping their monstrous jowls over the fattening of the Earth. They have awaited the proper setting of the banquet table and now they are dining.

"Their thoughts are not our thoughts, their ideals not our ideals. Perhaps they have nothing in common with us except the primal basis of all life, self-preservation, the necessity of feeding.

"Maybe they have come of their own will. I prefer to believe that they have. Perhaps they are merely following the natural course of events, obeying some immutable law legislated by some higher being who watches over the cosmos and dictates what shall be and what shall not be. If this is true it means that there has been a flaw in my reasoning, for I believed that the life of each plane degenerated in company with the degeneration of its plane of existence, which would obey the same evolutional laws which govern the life upon it. I am quite satisfied that this invasion is a well-planned campaign, that some fourth-dimensional race has found a means of breaking through the veil of force which separates its plane from ours."

"But," pointed out Henry Woods, "you say they are fourth-dimensional things. I can't see anything about them to suggest an additional dimension. They are plainly three-dimensional."

"Of course they are three-dimensional. They would have to be to live in this world of three dimensions. The only two-dimensional objects which we know of in this world are merely illusions, projections of the third dimension, like a shadow. It is impossible for more than one dimension to live on any single plane.

"To attack us they would have to lose one dimension. This they have evidently done. You can see how utterly ridiculous it would be for you to try to attack a two-dimensional thing. So far as you were concerned it would have no mass. The same is true of the other dimensions. Similarly a being of a lesser plane could not harm an inhabitant of a higher plane. It is apparent that while the Horror has lost one material dimension, it has retained certain fourth-dimensional properties which make it invulnerable to the forces at the command of our plane."

The newspaperman was now sitting on the edge of his chair.

"But," he asked breathlessly, "it all sounds so hopeless. What can be done about it?"

Dr. White hitched his chair closer and his fingers closed with a fierce grasp upon the other's knee. A militant boom came into his voice.

"My boy," he said, "we are to strike back. We are going to invade the fourth-dimensional plane of these hellhounds. We are going to make them feel our strength. We are going to strike back."

Henry Woods sprang to his feet.

"How?" he shouted. "Have you...?"

Dr. White nodded.

"I have found a way to send the third-dimensional into the fourth. Come and I will show you."

The machine was huge, but it had an appearance of simple construction. A large rectangular block of what appeared to be a strange black metal was set on end and flanked on each side by two smaller ones. On the top of the large block was set a half-globe of a strange substance, somewhat, Henry thought, like frosted glass. On one side of the large cube was set a lever, a long glass panel, two vertical tubes and three clock-face indicators. The control board, it appeared, was relatively simple.

Beside the mass of the five rectangles, on the floor, was a large plate of transparent substance, ground to a concave surface, through which one could see an intricate tangle of wire mesh.

Hanging from the ceiling, directly above the one on the floor, was another concave disk, but this one had a far more pronounced curvature.

Wires connected the two disks and each in turn was connected to the rectangular machine.

"It is a matter of the proper utilization of two forces, electrical and gravitational," proudly explained Dr. White. "Those two forces, properly used, warp the third-dimensional into the fourth. A reverse process is used to return the object to the third. The principle of the machine is—"

The old man was about to launch into a lengthy discussion, but Henry interrupted him. A glance at his watch had shown him press time was drawing perilously close.

"Just a second," he said. "You propose to warp a third-dimensional being into a fourth dimension. How can a third-dimensional thing exist there? You said a short time ago that only a specified dimension could exist on one single plane."

"You have missed my point," snapped Dr. White. "I am not sending a third-dimensional thing to a fourth dimension. I am changing the third-dimensional being into a fourth-dimensional being. I add a dimension, and automatically the being exists on a different plane. I am reversing evolution. This third dimension we now exist on evolved, millions of eons ago, from a fourth dimension. I am sending a lesser entity back over those millions of eons to a plane similar to one upon which his ancestors lived inconceivably long ago."

"But, man, how do you know you can do it?"

The doctor's eyes gleamed and his fingers reached out to press a bell.

A servant appeared almost at once.

"Bring me a dog," snapped the old man. The servant disappeared.

"Young man," said Dr. White, "I am going to show you how I know I can do it. I have done it before, now I am going to do it for you. I have sent dogs and cats back to the fourth dimension and returned them safely to this room. I can do the same with men."

The servant reappeared, carrying in his arms a small dog. The doctor stepped to the control board of his strange machine.

"All right, George," he said.

The servant had evidently worked with the old man enough to know what was expected of him. He stepped close to the floor disk and waited. The dog whined softly, sensing that all was not exactly right.

The old scientist slowly shoved the lever toward the right, and as he did so a faint hum filled the room, rising to a stupendous roar as he advanced the lever. From both floor disk and upper disk leaped strange cones of blue light, which met midway to form an hour-glass shape of brilliance.

The light did not waver or sparkle. It did not glow. It seemed hard and brittle, like straight bars of force. The newspaperman, gazing with awe upon it, felt that terrific force was there. What had the old man said? Warp a third-dimensional being into another dimension! That would take force!

As he watched, petrified by the spectacle, the servant stepped forward and, with a flip, tossed the little dog into the blue light. The animal could be discerned for a moment through the light and then it disappeared.

"Look in the globe!" shouted the old man; and Henry jerked his eyes from the column of light to the half-globe atop the machine.

He gasped. In the globe, deep within its milky center, glowed a picture that made his brain reel as he looked upon it. It was a scene such as no man could have imagined unaided. It was a horribly distorted projection of an eccentric landscape, a landscape hardly analogous to anything on Earth.

"That's the fourth dimension, sir," said the servant.

"That's not the fourth dimension," the old man corrected him. "That's a third-dimensional impression of the fourth dimension. It is no more the fourth dimension than a shadow is three-dimensional. It, like a shadow, is merely a projection. It gives us a glimpse of what the fourth plane is like. It is a shadow of that plane."

Slowly a dark blotch began to grow in the landscape. Slowly it assumed definite form. It puzzled the reporter. It looked familiar. He could have sworn he had seen it somewhere before. It was alive, for it had moved.

"That, sir, is the dog," George volunteered.

"That was the dog," Dr. White again corrected him. "God knows what it is now."

He turned to the newspaperman.

"Have you seen enough?" he demanded.

Henry nodded.

The other slowly began to return the lever to its original position. The roaring subsided, the light faded, the projection in the half-globe grew fainter.

"How are you going to use it?" asked the newspaperman.

"I have ninety-eight men who have agreed to be projected into the fourth dimension to seek out the entities that are attacking us and attack them in turn. I shall send them out in an hour."

"Where is there a phone?" asked the newspaperman.

"In the next room," replied Dr. White.

As the reporter dashed out of the door, the light faded entirely from between the two disks and on the lower one a little dog crouched, quivering, softly whimpering.

The old man stepped from the controls and approached the disk. He scooped the little animal from where it lay into his arms and patted the silky head.

"Good dog," he murmured; and the creature snuggled close to him, comforted, already forgetting that horrible place from which it had just returned.

"Is everything ready, George?" asked the old man.

"Yes, sir," replied the servant. "The men are all ready, even anxious to go. If you ask me, sir, they are a tough lot."

"They are as brave a group of men as ever graced the Earth," replied the scientist gently. "They are adventurers, every one of whom has faced danger and will not shrink from it. They are born fighters. My one regret is that I have not been able to secure more like them. A thousand men such as they should be able to conquer any opponent. It was impossible. The others were poor soft fools. They laughed in my face. They thought I was an old fool—I, the man who alone stands between them and utter destruction."

His voice had risen to almost a scream, but it again sank to a normal tone.

"I may be sending ninety-eight brave men to instant death. I hope not."

"You can always jerk them back, sir," suggested George.

"Maybe I can, maybe not," murmured the old man.

Henry Woods appeared in the doorway.

"When do we start?" he asked.

"We?" exclaimed the scientist.

"Certainly, you don't believe you're going to leave me out of this. Why, man, it's the greatest story of all time. I'm going as special war correspondent."

"They believed it? They are going to publish it?" cried the old man, clutching at the newspaperman's sleeve.

"Well, the editor was skeptical at first, but after I swore on all sorts of oaths it was true, he ate it up. Maybe you think that story didn't stop the presses!"

"I didn't expect them to. I just took a chance. I thought they, too, would laugh at me."

"But when do we start?" persisted Henry.

"You are really in earnest? You really want to go?" asked the old man, unbelievingly.

"I am going. Try to stop me."

Dr. White glanced at his watch.

"We will start in exactly thirty-four minutes," he said.

"Ten seconds to go." George, standing with watch in hand, spoke in a precise manner, the very crispness of his words betraying the excitement under which he labored.

The blue light, hissing, drove from disk to disk; the room thundered with the roar of the machine, before which stood Dr. White, his hand on the lever, his eyes glued on the instruments before him.

In a line stood the men who were to fling themselves into the light to be warped into another dimension, there to seek out and fight an unknown enemy. The line was headed by a tall man with hands like hams, with a weather-beaten face and a wild mop of hair. Behind him stood a belligerent little cockney. Henry Woods stood fifth in line. They were a motley lot, adventurers every one of them, and some were obviously afraid as they stood before that column of light, with only a few seconds of the third dimension left to them. They had answered a weird advertisement, and had but a limited idea of what they were about to do. Grimly, though, they accepted it as a job, a bizarre job, but a job. They faced it as they had faced other equally dangerous, but less unusual, jobs.

"Five seconds," snapped George.

The lever was all the way over now. The half-globe showed, within its milky interior, a hideously distorted landscape. The light had taken on a hard, brittle appearance and its hiss had risen to a scream. The machine thundered steadily with a suggestion of horrible power.

"Time up!"

The tall man stepped forward. His foot reached the disk; another step and he was bathed in the light, a third and he glimmered momentarily, then vanished. Close on his heels followed the little cockney.

With his nerves at almost a snapping point, Henry moved on behind the fourth man. He was horribly afraid, he wanted to break from the line and run, it didn't matter where, any place to get away from that steady, steely light in front of him. He had seen three men step into it, glow for a second, and then disappear. A fourth man had placed his foot on the disk.

Cold sweat stood out on his brow. Like an automaton he placed one foot on the disk. The fourth man had already disappeared.

"Snap into it, pal," growled the man behind.

Henry lifted the other foot, caught his toe on the edge of the disk and stumbled headlong into the column of light.

He was conscious of intense heat which was instantly followed by equally intense cold. For a moment his body seemed to be under enormous pressure, then it seemed to be expanding, flying apart, bursting, exploding....

He felt solid ground under his feet, and his eyes, snapping open, saw an alien land. It was a land of somber color, with great gray moors, and beetling black cliffs. There was something queer about it, an intangible quality that baffled him.

He looked about him, expecting to see his companions. He saw no one. He was absolutely alone in that desolate brooding land. Something dreadful had happened! Was he the only one to be safely transported from the third dimension? Had some horrible accident occurred? Was he alone?

Sudden panic seized him. If something had happened, if the others were not here, might it not be possible that the machine would not be able to bring him back to his own dimension? Was he doomed to remain marooned forever in this terrible plane?

He looked down at his body and gasped in dismay. It was not his body!

It was a grotesque caricature of a body, a horrible profane mass of flesh, like a phantasmagoric beast snatched from the dreams of a lunatic.

It was real, however. He felt it with his hands, but they were not hands. They were something like hands; they served the same purpose that hands served in the third dimension. He was, he realized, a being of the fourth dimension, but in his fourth-dimensional brain still clung hard-fighting remnants of that faithful old third-dimensional brain. He could not, as yet, see with fourth-dimensional eyes, think purely fourth-dimensional thoughts. He had not oriented himself as yet to this new plane of existence. He was seeing the fourth dimension through the blurred lenses of millions of eons of third-dimensional existence. He was seeing it much more clearly than he had seen it in the half-globe atop the machine in Dr. White's laboratory, but he would not see it clearly until every vestige of the third dimension was wiped from him. That, he knew, would come in time.

He felt his weird body with those things that served as hands, and he found, beneath his groping, unearthly fingers, great rolling muscles, powerful tendons, and hard, well-conditioned flesh. A sense of well-being surged through him and he growled like an animal, like an animal of that horrible fourth plane.

But the terrible sounds that came from between his slobbering lips were not those of his own voice, they were the voices of many men.

Then he knew. He was not alone. Here, in this one body were the bodies, the brains, the power, the spirit, of those other ninety-eight men. In the fourth dimension, all the millions of third-dimensional things were one. Perhaps that particular portion of the third dimension called the Earth had sprung from, or degenerated from, one single unit of a dissolving, worn-out fourth dimension. The third dimension, warped back to a higher plane, was automatically obeying the mystic laws of evolution by reforming in the shape of that old ancestor, unimaginably removed in time from the race he had begot. He was no longer Henry Woods, newspaperman; he was an entity that had given birth, in the dim ages when the Earth was born, to a third dimension. Nor was he alone. This body of his was composed of other sons of that ancient entity.

He felt himself grow, felt his body grow vaster, assume greater proportions, felt new vitality flow through him. It was the other men, the men who were flinging themselves into the column of light in the laboratory to be warped back to this plane, to be incorporated in his body.

It was not his body, however. His brain was not his alone. The pronoun, he realized, represented the sum total of those other men, his fellow adventurers.

Suddenly a new feeling came, a feeling of completeness, a feeling of supreme fitness. He knew that the last of the ninety-eight men had stepped across the disk, that all were here in this giant body.

Now he could see more clearly. Things in the landscape, which had escaped him before, became recognizable. Awful thoughts ran through his brain, heavy, ponderous, black thoughts. He began to recognize the landscape as something familiar, something he had seen before, a thing with which he was intimate. Phenomena, which his third-dimensional intelligence would have gasped at, became commonplace. He was finally seeing through fourth-dimensional eyes, thinking fourth-dimensional thoughts.

Memory seeped into his brain and he had fleeting visions, visions of dark caverns lit by hellish flames, of huge seas that battered remorselessly with mile-high waves against towering headlands that reared titanic toward a glowering sky. He remembered a red desert scattered with scarlet boulders, he remembered silver cliffs of gleaming metallic stone. Through all his thoughts ran something else, a scarlet thread of hate, an all-consuming passion, a fierce lust after the life of some other entity.

He was no longer a composite thing built of third-dimensional beings. He was a creature of another plane, a creature with a consuming hate, and suddenly he knew against whom this hate was directed and why. He knew also that this creature was near and his great fists closed and then spread wide as he knew it. How did he know it? Perhaps through some sense which he, as a being of another plane, held, but which was alien to the Earth. Later, he asked himself this question. At the time, however, there was no questioning on his part. He only knew that somewhere near was a hated enemy and he did not question the source of his knowledge....

Mumbling in an idiom incomprehensible to a third-dimensional being, filled with rage that wove redly through his brain, he lumbered down the hill onto the moor, his great strides eating up the distance, his footsteps shaking the ground.

At the foot of the hill he halted and from his throat issued a challenging roar that made the very crags surrounding the moor tremble. The rocks flung back the roar as if in mockery.

Again he shouted and in the shout he framed a lurid insult to the enemy that lurked there in the cliffs.

Again the crags flung back the insult, but this time the echoes, booming over the moor, were drowned by another voice, the voice of the enemy.

At the far end of the moor appeared a gigantic form, a form that shambled on grotesque, misshapen feet, growling angrily as he came.

He came rapidly despite his clumsy gait, and as he came he mouthed terrific threats.

Close to the other he halted and only then did recognition dawn in his eyes.

"You, Mal Shaff?" he growled in his guttural tongue, and surprise and consternation were written large upon his ugly face.

"Yes, it is I, Mal Shaff," boomed the other. "Remember, Ouglat, the day you destroyed me and my plane. I have returned to wreak my vengeance. I have solved a mystery you have never guessed and I have come back. You did not imagine you were attacking me again when you sent your minions to that other plane to feed upon the beings there. It was I you were attacking, fool, and I am here to kill you."

Ouglat leaped and the thing that had been Henry Woods, newspaperman, and ninety-eight other men, but was now Mal Shaff of the fourth dimension, leaped to meet him.

Mal Shaff felt the force of Ouglat, felt the sharp pain of a hammering fist, and lashed out with those horrible arms of his to smash at the leering face of his antagonist. He felt his fists strike solid flesh, felt the bones creak and tremble beneath his blow.

His nostrils were filled with the terrible stench of the other's foul breath and his filthy body. He teetered on his gnarled legs and side-stepped a vicious kick and then stepped in to gouge with straightened thumb at the other's eye. The thumb went true and Ouglat howled in pain.

Mal Shaff leaped back as his opponent charged head down, and his knotted fist beat a thunderous tattoo as the misshapen beast closed in. He felt clawing fingers seeking his throat, felt ghastly nails ripping at his shoulders. In desperation he struck blindly, and Ouglat reeled away. With a quick stride he shortened the distance between them and struck Ouglat a hard blow squarely on his slavering mouth. Pressing hard upon the reeling figure, he swung his fists like sledge-hammers, and Ouglat stumbled, falling in a heap on the sand.

Mal Shaff leaped upon the fallen foe and kicked him with his taloned feet, ripping him wickedly. There was no thought of fair play, no faintest glimmer of mercy. This was a battle to the death: there could be no quarter.

The fallen monster howled, but his voice cut short as his foul mouth, with its razor-edged fangs, closed on the other's body. His talons, seeking a hold, clawed deep.

Mal Shaff, his brain a screaming maelstrom of weird emotions, aimed pile-driver blows at the enemy, clawed and ripped. Together the two rolled, locked tight in titanic battle, on the sandy plain and a great cloud of heavy dust marked where they struggled.

In desperation Ouglat put every ounce of his strength into a heave that broke the other's grip and flung him away.

The two monstrosities surged to their feet, their eyes red with hate, glaring through the dust cloud at one another.

Slowly Ouglat's hand stole to a black, wicked cylinder that hung on a belt at his waist. His fingers closed upon it and he drew the weapon. As he leveled it at Mal Shaff, his lips curled back and his features distorted into something that was not pleasant to see.

Mal Shaff, with doubled fists, saw the great thumb of his enemy slowly depressing a button on the cylinder, and a great fear held him rooted in his tracks. In the back of his brain something was vainly trying to explain to him the horror of this thing which the other held.

Then a multicolored spiral, like a corkscrew column of vapor, sprang from the cylinder and flashed toward him. It struck him full on the chest and even as it did so he caught the ugly fire of triumph in the red eyes of his enemy.

He felt a stinging sensation where the spiral struck, but that was all. He was astounded. He had feared this weapon, had been sure it portended some form of horrible death. But all it did was to produce a slight sting.

For a split second he stood stock-still, then he surged forward and advanced upon Ouglat, his hands outspread like claws. From his throat came those horrible sounds, the speech of the fourth dimension.

"Did I not tell you, foul son of Sargouthe, that I had solved a mystery you have never guessed at? Although you destroyed me long ago, I have returned. Throw away your puny weapon. I am of the lower dimension and am invulnerable to your engines of destruction. You bloated...." His words trailed off into a stream of vileness that could never have occurred to a third-dimensional mind.

Ouglat, with every line of his face distorted with fear, flung the weapon from him, and turning, fled clumsily down the moor, with Mal Shaff at his heels.

Steadily Mal Shaff gained and with only a few feet separating him from Ouglat, he dived with outspread arms at the other's legs.

The two came down together, but Mal Shaff's grip was broken by the fall and the two regained their feet at almost the same instant.

The wild moor resounded to their throaty roaring and the high cliffs flung back the echoes of the bellowing of the two gladiators below. It was sheer strength now and flesh and bone were bruised and broken under the life-shaking blows that they dealt. Great furrows were plowed in the sand by the sliding of heavy feet as the two fighters shifted to or away from attack. Blood, blood of fourth-dimensional creatures, covered the bodies of the two and stained the sand with its horrible hue. Perspiration streamed from them and their breath came in gulping gasps.

The lurid sun slid across the purple sky and still the two fought on. Ouglat, one of the ancients, and Mal Shaff, reincarnated. It was a battle of giants, a battle that must have beggared even the titanic tilting of forgotten gods and entities in the ages when the third-dimensional Earth was young.

Mal Shaff had no conception of time. He may have fought seconds or hours. It seemed an eternity. He had attempted to fight scientifically, but had failed to do so. While one part of him had cried out to elude his opponent, to wait for openings, to conserve his strength, another part had shouted at him to step in and smash, smash, smash at the hated monstrosity pitted against him.

It seemed Ouglat was growing in size, had become more agile, that his strength was greater. His punches hurt more; it was harder to hit him.

Still Mal Shaff drilled in determinedly, head down, fists working like pistons. As the other seemed to grow stronger and larger, he seemed to become smaller and weaker.

It was queer. Ouglat should be tired, too. His punches should be weaker. He should move more slowly, be heavier on his feet.

There was no doubt of it. Ouglat was growing larger, was drawing on some mysterious reserve of strength. From somewhere new force and life were flowing into his body. But from where was this strength coming?

A huge fist smashed against Mal Shaff's jaw. He felt himself lifted, and the next moment he skidded across the sand.

Lying there, gasping for breath, almost too fagged to rise, with the black bulk of the enemy looming through the dust cloud before him, he suddenly realized the source of the other's renewed strength.

Ouglat was recalling his minions from the third dimension! They were incorporating in his body, returning to their parent body!

They were coming back from the third dimension to the fourth dimension to fight a third-dimensional thing reincarnated in the fourth-dimensional form it had lost millions of eons ago!

This was the end, thought Mal Shaff. But he staggered to his feet to meet the charge of the ancient enemy and a grim song, a death chant immeasurably old, suddenly and dimly remembered from out of the mists of countless millenniums, was on his lips as he swung a pile-driver blow into the suddenly astonished face of the rushing Ouglat....

The milky globe atop the machine in Dr. White's laboratory glowed softly, and within that glow two figures seemed to struggle.

Before the machine, his hands still on the controls, stood Dr. Silas White. Behind him the room was crowded with newspapermen and photographers.

Hours had passed since the ninety-eight men—ninety-nine, counting Henry Woods—had stepped into the brittle column of light to be shunted back through unguessed time to a different plane of existence. The old scientist, during all those hours, had stood like a graven image before his machine, eyes staring fixedly at the globe.

Through the open windows he had heard the cry of the newsboy as the Press put the greatest scoop of all time on the street. The phone had rung like mad and George answered it. The doorbell buzzed repeatedly and George ushered in newspapermen who had asked innumerable questions, to which he had replied briefly, almost mechanically. The reporters had fought for the use of the one phone in the house and had finally drawn lots for it. A few had raced out to use other phones.

Photographers came and flashes popped and cameras clicked. The room was in an uproar. On the rare occasions when the reporters were not using the phone the instrument buzzed shrilly. Authoritative voices demanded Dr. Silas White. George, his eyes on the old man, stated that Dr. Silas White could not be disturbed, that he was busy.

From the street below came the heavy-throated hum of thousands of voices. The street was packed with a jostling crowd of awed humanity, every eye fastened on the house of Dr. Silas White. Lines of police held them back.

"What makes them move so slowly?" asked a reporter, staring at the globe. "They hardly seem to be moving. It looks like a slow motion picture."

"They are not moving slowly," replied Dr. White. "There must be a difference in time in the fourth dimension. Maybe what is hours to us is only seconds to them. Time must flow more slowly there. Perhaps it is a bigger place than this third plane. That may account for it. They aren't moving slowly, they are fighting savagely. It's a fight to the death! Watch!"

The grotesque arm of one of the figures in the milky globe was moving out slowly, loafing along, aimed at the head of the other. Slowly the other twisted his body aside, but too slowly. The fist finally touched the head, still moving slowly forward, the body following as slowly. The head of the creature twisted, bent backward, and the body toppled back in a leisurely manner.

"What does White say?... Can't you get a statement of some sort from him? Won't he talk at all? A hell of a fine reporter you are—can't even get a man to open his mouth. Ask him about Henry Woods. Get a human-interest slant on Woods walking into the light. Ask him how long this is going to last. Damn it all, man, do something, and don't bother me again until you have a real story—yes, I said a real story—are you hard of hearing? For God's sake, do something!"

The editor slammed the receiver on the hook.

"Brooks," he snapped, "get the War Department at Washington. Ask them if they're going to back up White. Go on, go on. Get busy.... How will you get them? I don't know. Just get them, that's all. Get them!"

Typewriters gibbered like chuckling morons through the roaring tumult of the editorial rooms. Copy boys rushed about, white sheets clutched in their grimy hands. Telephones jangled and strident voices blared through the haze that arose from the pipes and cigarettes of perspiring writers who feverishly transferred to paper the startling events that were rocking the world.

The editor, his necktie off, his shirt open, his sleeves rolled to the elbow, drummed his fingers on the desk. It had been a hectic twenty-four hours and he had stayed at the desk every minute of the time. He was dead tired. When the moment of relaxation came, when the tension snapped, he knew he would fall into an exhausted stupor of sleep, but the excitement was keeping him on his feet. There was work to do. There was news such as the world had never known before. Each new story meant a new front make-up, another extra. Even now the presses were thundering, even now papers with the ink hardly dry upon them were being snatched by the avid public from the hands of screaming newsboys.

A man raced toward the city desk, waving a sheet of paper in his hand. Sensing something unusual the others in the room crowded about as he laid the sheet before the editor.

"Just came in," the man gasped.

The paper was a wire dispatch. It read:

"Rome—The Black Horror is in full retreat. Although still apparently immune to the weapons being used against it, it is lifting the siege of this city. The cause is unknown."

The editor ran his eye down the sheet. There was another dateline:

"Madrid—The Black Horror, which has enclosed this city in a ring of dark terror for the last two days, is fleeing, rapidly disappearing...."

The editor pressed a button. There was an answering buzz.

"Composing room," he shouted, "get ready for a new front! Yes, another extra. This will knock their eyes out!"

A telephone jangled furiously. The editor seized it.

"Yes. What was that?... White says he must have help. I see. Woods and the others are weakening. Being badly beaten, eh?... More men needed to go out to the other plane. Wants reinforcements. Yes. I see. Well, tell him that he'll have them. If he can wait half an hour we'll have them walking by thousands into that light. I'll be damned if we won't! Just tell White to hang on! We'll have the whole nation coming to the rescue!"

He jabbed up the receiver.

"Richards," he said, "write a streamer, 'Help Needed,' 'Reinforcements Called'—something of that sort, you know. Make it scream. Tell the foreman to dig out the biggest type he has. A foot high. If we ever needed big type, we need it now!"

He turned to the telephone.

"Operator," he said, "get me the Secretary of War at Washington. The secretary in person, you understand. No one else will do."

He turned again to the reporters who stood about the desk.

"In two hours," he explained, banging the desk top for emphasis, "we'll have the United States Army marching into that light Woods walked into!"

The bloody sun was touching the edge of the weird world, seeming to hesitate before taking the final plunge behind the towering black crags that hung above the ink-pot shadows at their base. The purple sky had darkened until it was almost the color of soft, black velvet. Great stars were blazing out.

Ouglat loomed large in the gathering twilight, a horrible misshapen ogre of an outer world. He had grown taller, broader, greater. Mal Shaff's head now was on a level with the other's chest; his huge arms seemed toylike in comparison with those of Ouglat, his legs mere pipestems.

Time and time again he had barely escaped as the clutching hands of Ouglat reached out to grasp him. Once within those hands he would be torn apart.

The battle had become a game of hide and seek, a game of cat and mouse, with Mal Shaff the mouse.

Slowly the sun sank and the world became darker. His brain working feverishly, Mal Shaff waited for the darkness. Adroitly he worked the battle nearer and nearer to the Stygian darkness that lay at the foot of the mighty crags. In the darkness he might escape. He could no longer continue this unequal fight. Only escape was left.

The sun was gone now. Blackness was dropping swiftly over the land, like a great blanket, creating the illusion of the glowering sky descending to the ground. Only a few feet away lay the total blackness under the cliffs.

Like a flash Mal Shaff darted into the blackness, was completely swallowed in it. Roaring, Ouglat followed.

His shoulders almost touching the great rock wall that shot straight up hundreds of feet above him, Mal Shaff ran swiftly, fear lending speed to his shivering legs. Behind him he heard the bellowing of his enemy. Ouglat was searching for him, a hopeless search in that total darkness. He would never find him. Mal Shaff felt sure.

Fagged and out of breath, he dropped panting at the foot of the wall. Blood pounded through his head and his strength seemed to be gone. He lay still and stared out into the less dark moor that stretched before him.

For some time he lay there, resting. Aimlessly he looked out over the moor, and then he suddenly noted, some distance to his right, a hill rising from the moor. The hill was vaguely familiar. He remembered it dimly as being of great importance.

A sudden inexplicable restlessness filled him. Far behind him he heard the enraged bellowing of

Ouglat, but that he scarcely noticed. So long as darkness lay upon the land he knew he was safe from his enemy.

The hill had made him restless. He must reach the top. He could think of no logical reason for doing so. Obviously he was safer here at the base of the cliff, but a voice seemed to be calling, a friendly voice from the hilltop.

He rose on aching legs and forged ahead. Every fiber of his being cried out in protest, but resolutely he placed one foot ahead of the other, walking mechanically.

Opposite the hill he disregarded the strange call that pulsed down upon him, long enough to rest his tortured body. He must build up his strength for the climb.

He realized that danger lay ahead. Once he quitted the blackness of the cliff's base, Ouglat, even in the darkness that lay over the land, might see him. That would be disastrous. Once over the top of the hill he would be safe.

Suddenly the landscape was bathed in light, a soft green radiance. One moment it had been pitch dark, the next it was light, as if a giant search-light had been snapped on.

In terror, Mal Shaff looked for the source of the light. Just above the horizon hung a great green orb, which moved up the ladder of the sky even as he watched.

A moon! A huge green satellite hurtling swiftly around this cursed world!

A great, overwhelming fear sat upon Mal Shaff and with a high, shrill scream of anger he raced forward, forgetful of aching body and outraged lungs.

His scream was answered from far off, and out of the shadows of the cliffs toward the far end of the moor a black figure hurled itself. Ouglat was on the trail!

Mal Shaff tore madly up the slope, topped the crest, and threw himself flat on the ground, almost exhausted.

A queer feeling stole over him, a queer feeling of well-being. New strength was flowing into him, the old thrill of battle was pounding through his blood once more.

Not only were queer things happening to his body, but also to his brain. The world about him looked queer, held a sort of an intangible mystery he could not understand. A half question formed in the back of his brain. Who and what was he? Queer thoughts to be thinking! He was Mal Shaff, but had he always been Mal Shaff?

He remembered a brittle column of light, creatures with bodies unlike his body, walking into it. He had been one of those creatures. There was something about dimensions, about different planes, a plan for one plane to attack another!

He scrambled to his bowed legs and beat his great chest with mighty, long-nailed hands. He flung back his head and from his throat broke a sound to curdle the blood of even the bravest.

On the moor below Ouglat heard the cry and answered it with one equally ferocious.

Mal Shaff took a step forward, then stopped stock-still. Through his brain went a sharp command to return to the spot where he had stood, to wait there until attacked. He stepped back, shifting his feet impatiently.

He was growing larger; every second fresh vitality was pouring into him. Before his eyes danced a red curtain of hate and his tongue roared forth a series of insulting challenges to the figure that was even now approaching the foot of the hill.

As Ouglat climbed the hill, the night became an insane bedlam. The challenging roars beat like surf against the black cliffs.

Ouglat's lips were flecked with foam, his red eyes were mere slits, his mouth worked convulsively.

They were only a few feet apart when Ouglat charged.

Mal Shaff was ready for him. There was no longer any difference in their size and they met like the two forward walls of contending football teams.

Mal Shaff felt the soft throat of the other under his fingers and his grip tightened. Maddened,

Ouglat shot terrific blow after terrific blow into Mal Shaff's body.

Try as he might, however, he could not shake the other's grip.

It was silent now. The night seemed brooding, watching the struggle on the hilltop.

Larger and larger grew Mal Shaff, until he overtopped Ouglat like a giant.

Then he loosened his grip and, as Ouglat tried to scuttle away, reached down to grasp him by the nape of his neck.

High above his head he lifted his enemy and dashed him to the ground. With a leap he was on the prostrate figure, trampling it apart, smashing it into the ground. With wild cries he stamped the earth, treading out the last of Ouglat, the Black Horror.

When no trace of the thing that had been Ouglat remained, he moved away and viewed the trampled ground.

Then, for the first time he noticed that the crest of the hill was crowded with other monstrous figures. He glared at them, half in surprise, half in anger. He had not noticed their silent approach.

"It is Mal Shaff!" cried one.

"Yes, I am Mal Shaff. What do you want?"

"But, Mal Shaff, Ouglat destroyed you once long ago!"

"And I, just now," replied Mal Shaff, "have destroyed Ouglat."

The figures were silent, shifting uneasily. Then one stepped forward.

"Mal Shaff," it said, "we thought you were dead. Apparently it was not so. We welcome you to our land again. Ouglat, who once tried to kill you and apparently failed, you have killed, which is right and proper. Come and live with us again in peace. We welcome you."

Mal Shaff bowed.

Gone was all thought of the third dimension. Through Mal Shaff's mind raced strange, haunting memories of a red desert scattered with scarlet boulders, of silver cliffs of gleaming metallic stone, of huge seas battering against towering headlands. There were other things, too. Great palaces of shining jewels, and weird nights of inhuman joy where hellish flames lit deep, black caverns.

He bowed again.

"I thank you, Bathazar," he said.

Without a backward look he shambled down the hill with the others.

"Yes?" said the editor. "What's that you say? Doctor White is dead! A suicide! Yeah, I understand. Worry, hey! Here, Roberts, take this story."

He handed over the phone.

"When you write it," he said, "play up the fact he was worried about not being able to bring the men back to the third dimension. Give him plenty of praise for ending the Black Horror. It's a big story."

"Sure," said Roberts, then spoke into the phone: "All right, Bill, shoot the works."